Stella Batts

Needs a New Name

Praise for Stella Batts:

"Sheinmel has a great ear for the dialogue and concerns of eight-year-old girls. Bell's artwork is breezy and light, reflecting the overall tone of the book. This would be a good choice for fans of Barbara Park's 'Junie B. Jones' books."
—*School Library Journal*

"First in a series featuring eight-year-old Stella, Sheinmel's unassuming story, cheerily illustrated by Bell, is a reliable read for those first encountering chapter books. With a light touch, Sheinmel persuasively conveys elementary school dynamics; readers may recognize some of their own inflated reactions to small mortifications in likeable Stella, while descriptions of unique candy confections are mouth-watering."
— *Publisher's Weekly*

Other books in this series:

Stella Batts, Hair Today, Gone Tomorrow

Stella Batts Pardon Me

Stella Batts A Case of the Meanies

Stella Batts Who's in Charge?

Meet Stella and friends online at www.stellabatts.com

Stella Batts

Needs a New Name

Book

1

Courtney Sheinmel

Illustrated by Jennifer A. Bell

For Sara Nicole and Tesa Ny, with so much love
(and special thanks to Maverick Atticus)
—Courtney

For my sister Kris
—Jennifer

Text Copyright © 2012 Courtney Sheinmel
Illustrations Copyright © 2012 Jennifer A. Bell

Sleeping Bear Press™

315 East Eisenhower Parkway, Suite 200 • Ann Arbor, MI 48108 • www.sleepingbearpress.com
© 2012 Sleeping Bear Press

Printed and bound in the United States.
10 9 8 7 6 5 4 3

Library of Congress Cataloging-in-Publication Data • Sheinmel, Courtney. • Stella Batts needs a new name / by Courtney Sheinmel. • p. cm. • Summary: When a classmate makes fun of her name, eight-year-old Stella picks a new one for herself, but discovers that the name she abandoned suits her just fine. • ISBN 978-1-58536-185-4 (hard cover) – ISBN 978-1-58536-183-0 (pbk.) • [1. Names, Personal–Fiction. 2. Nicknames–Fiction 3. Teasing–Fiction. 4. Schools–Fiction. 5. Family life–Fiction.] I. Title. • PZ7.S54124Ste 2012 • [Fic]–dc23 • 2011032119

Table of Contents

(that means some background at the beginning of the story):

My name is Stella Batts. I'm going to be a writer when I grow up, because writing is one of my favorite things. Except I'm not waiting until I grow up, because this is my first book. It's going to be an autobiography. That means I'm writing it and it's all about me. I am eight years old. I live in California. I was born at a hospital in a city called San Francisco, and now I live in a house in a town called Somers. You say it like "summers."

My favorite place in Somers is my parents' candy store, which is called Batts Confections. "Confections" is just a big word that means candy. They sell M&Ms, gumdrops, jelly beans, toffee, and basically any other sweet you can imagine. There's also a special fudge counter. The fudge is made at our store—and it's called Stella's Fudge. It was named after me because fudge is one of my favorite things to eat. I know how to make it too, but I'm not allowed to write it here because it's our family's secret recipe.

Here are some of my other favorite things:

1. The color yellow
2. Using big words
3. Dolphins
4. Getting to press the buttons in elevators
5. Making lists

When this book is finished it's going to be in all the bookstores and anyone can buy it. It'll say "By Stella Batts" in big letters on the cover. I'll be famous and people will know my name.

Except my name is not one of my favorite things.

Last week something happened on our class nature walk that I don't really want to write about—this is my book, so I get to pick what's in it.

But afterwards, this boy in my class named Joshua called me Smella. He would've

never said what he did if I was born with a different name. Also I think maybe if I had another name, it would look better on the cover of a book.

I'm not sure what else I should write so that will be the end of my introduction.

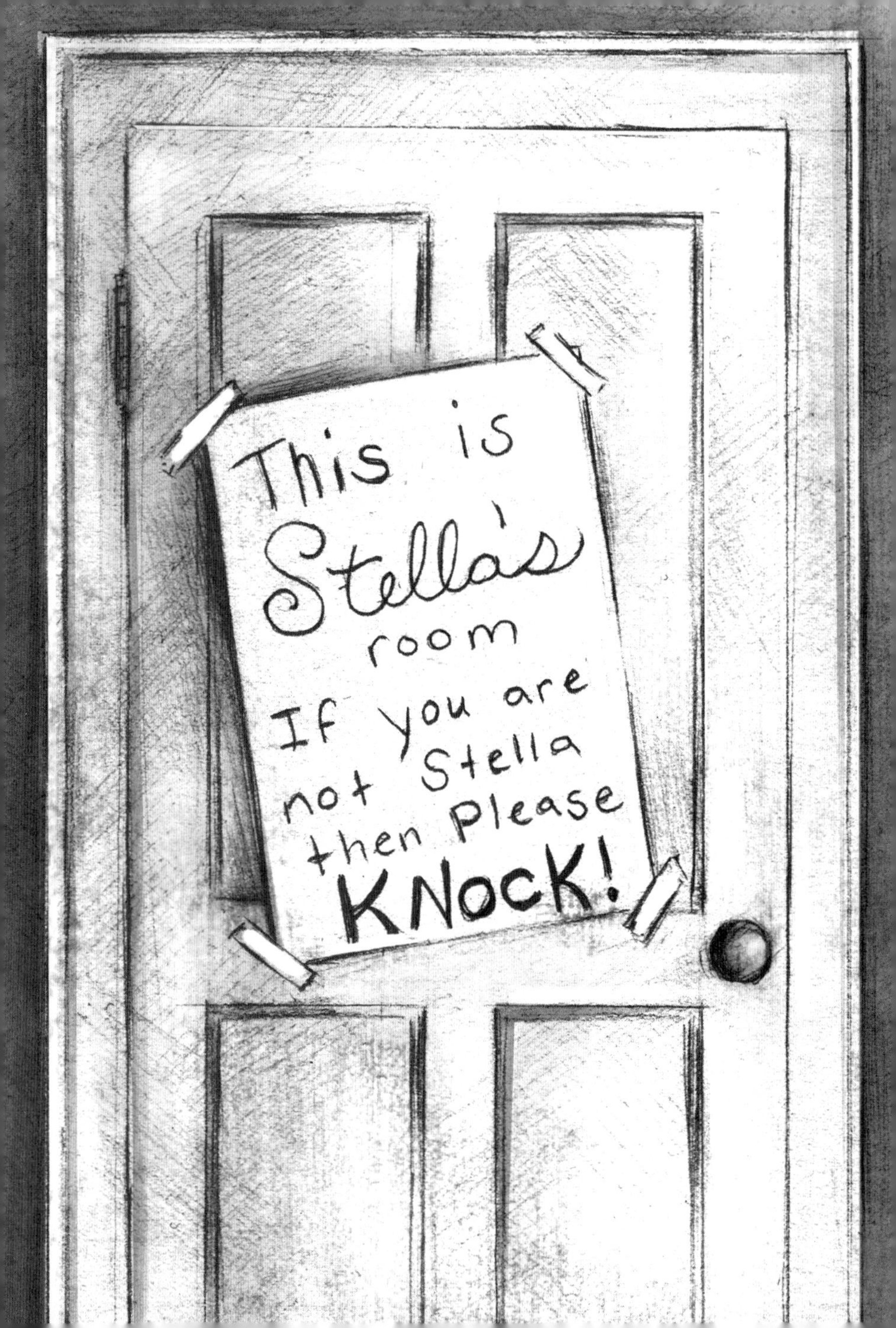
This is
Stella's
room
If you are
not Stella
then Please
KNOCK!

CHAPTER 1

It's Not Fair

My sister Penny came into my room without knocking, even though there's a sign on the door that says: *This is Stella's Room. If You Are Not Stella Then Please Knock.* I made the sign myself. It's on yellow construction paper. We have a package of construction paper in all different colors. I always pick yellow until those sheets run out.

Penny isn't a good reader yet because she's only five, but she knows what my sign says because I've told her.

"Guess what! My tongue is purple!" Penny announced.

"You have to knock first," I reminded her.

"I forgot," Penny said. She turned around and walked back out. Then she knocked on the door.

"Who is it?" I asked.

"It's me, Penny," Penny said.

"Thank you for knocking," I said. My parents get mad if Penny and I don't say *please* and *thank you.* "You can come in." So Penny came back in. She was carrying Belinda.

Belinda's not a person, she's a stuffed animal. A duck-billed platypus stuffed animal, if you want to know. It's Penny's favorite toy because the boy named Maverick who lives next door gave it to her, and Penny always calls Maverick her boyfriend.

Right then Penny was in her pajamas. She gets ready for bed before I do because her bedtime is a half hour before mine.

"My tongue is still purple from the Candy Marker," Penny said.

Candy Markers are a new kind of treat from Batts Confections. Dad brought them home so Penny and I could test them out at dessert. They come in all different flavors— each flavor is a different color. Purple is grape. You can paint your tongue with them, and then your tongue tastes really yummy. I had a cherry one, which made my tongue red— super red, not just regular red like tongues usually are.

"What are you doing?" Penny asked.

"I'm writing a book," I said.

"Neat-o," Penny said. "Let me see."

"No," I said.

"Why?" she asked.

"Because it's my book," I told her. "I don't want to show it to anyone until I'm finished. Like when you go into a bookstore, you don't get to see the books until they're already written."

"It's not fair," Penny said. That's what she says whenever I don't include her in stuff.

Penny stomped out of my room. I knew she was going to tell on me. That's what five-year-old sisters do. And I was right, because she came back in with Mom.

"I didn't do anything wrong," I told Mom

right away.

Mom sat down on my bed. Penny stuck her purple tongue out at me, but Mom didn't see.

"Mom!" I said. "Penny stuck out her tongue! That's not allowed."

"I was just showing you it was still purple," Penny said.

So then I stuck my tongue out at Penny.

"Oh, Stel," Mom said.

"I was just showing her mine was still really red," I explained.

"All right, enough of that," Mom said. "Penny says you're writing a book."

"That's right, I am," I told her. "I want to be a writer."

"Me too," Penny said. "I'm going to be a princess, and a candy store owner, and a writer."

"That's too many things," I said.

"No it's not," Penny said. "Right, Mom?"

"You'll be very busy, but I'm sure you can do it all," Mom told her.

"She didn't want to be a writer until I said I wanted to. She always copies me," I complained. Sometimes I like Penny to copy me, but sometimes I don't.

"Imitation is the sincerest form of flattery," Mom said. She says that whenever I get upset about Penny trying to be like me. Imitation is another word for copying and flattery is like saying something nice about someone.

"But I can't write as fast as Stella can," Penny whined.

"Maybe Stella can help you tomorrow," Mom said.

I shrugged. "Maybe," I said. I was still mad about Penny telling on me and then sticking out her tongue.

"Why don't you make Stella help me now?" Penny asked.

"Because now it's time for you to go to bed," Mom told her.

"I don't have to take a bath so I still have time," Penny told her. Mom's rule is that Penny and I have to take baths every other night.

"You're right about the bath, you're wrong about the time," Mom told her.

"Okay, but I have to go to the bathroom first, and you have to flush," Penny said. Penny is afraid to flush the toilet. She thinks maybe she'll get sucked in if she stands too close while the water is going down. Mom says I was the same way when I was little, but I'm not sure because I don't remember that at all.

"Okay," Mom said. "And then you have to brush your teeth and then pick out a story."

"Hey, Mom, guess what," Penny said.

"What?" Mom asked.

"I can brush my teeth and dance at the same time," Penny told her.

"I can't wait to see," Mom said. Then she turned to me. "And you, my little writer, have ten minutes left before you have to change into pajamas."

"Maybe I'll take a bath," I said.

"Oh honey, you really don't have enough

time," Mom said.

"Are you sure?" I asked her. "I think I might need one."

"You took one last night," Mom said. "You're still clean. Here, help me up." She held out her hand. I stood up and grabbed it. Even with me helping, Mom still needed to push her other hand down on the bed. She stood up very slowly and said "Ahhh." Then she and Penny walked out of the room, and I sat back down at my desk.

The reason why it's hard for Mom to get up is because she's pregnant. Mom and Dad say the baby will be born in a month and a half. They also say it's going to be a boy named Theodore. We are going to call him Teddy for short. Teddy is a nickname for Theodore, even though it doesn't really sound like it is.

Penny is a nickname, too. Her real name is Penelope.

I don't have a nickname. Sometimes people call me Stel, but that's not the same thing. It's not a real nickname. Smella is definitely NOT a nickname.

Okay, I'll write about what happened on the nature walk, but not the whole thing. Our teacher, Mrs. Finkel, told us to hurry up,

so then I did, but I tripped and fell over this branch. I don't even want to say what I landed in, it was too gross, so I'm going to leave out that part. Then Joshua was laughing and that's when he started calling me Smella. I'm not a smelly girl, or anything like that. But I thought maybe I should take a bath tonight, just in case.

I hate that he can make up something like

that about my name. I hate that Stel rhymes with Smell. I don't really like the name Stella at all anymore.

I think it would be good to have a name that had a real nickname. Penelope is a way better name—it sounds kind of sing-songy, and Penny is the perfect nickname for it. But Stella isn't a sing-songy name. It only has two syllables, and it doesn't have any good nicknames. I got to be the older sister, but Penny got to have the best name.

It's not fair, I said when Mom and Penny had left the room. But I said it in my head, not out loud like Penny does. Then I stood up and clicked my heels together three times. That's what I do if I'm making a wish. I got it from the movie *The Wizard of Oz.* In the movie, the girl named Dorothy clicked her heels together when she wanted to go home.

I think that trick might work for wishes, too.

After that, Mom came back in my room and said it was time for me to get ready for bed. I was done with my first chapter so it was a good time to take a break anyway.

CHAPTER 2

Fill in the Mrs. Blank

I'm going to write some stuff in my book about school. I'm in third grade, which means I'm in elementary school. Penny is in kindergarten. She's in elementary school too, but her class is in a different building for the little kids.

Like I said, my teacher's name is Mrs. Finkel. I know her first name is Dara because the other third-grade teacher, Mrs. Bower, sometimes pokes her head in the doorway of our classroom and says, "Are you coming to lunch today, Dara?" But of course I'm not allowed to call my teacher Dara. I call her Mrs. Finkel.

We have twenty-two kids in the class, including Willa and me. Willa is my best friend. We've been best friends since kindergarten. This is what happened: our kindergarten teacher, Mrs. Odesky, made everyone line up

in size order every day, and then we walked in a line down to the lunchroom. I was the shortest in class and Willa was second shortest, so we always stood next to each other.

We're really lucky because we've been in the same class every year since kindergarten. If I didn't have Willa in class with me, I'd want to be in Mrs. Bower's class, because everyone says she's not as strict as Mrs. Finkel.

Willa and I don't get to sit next to each other though. That's because on the first day of school this year, we had to line up in size order again. Then we got assigned our seats. The shortest kids sat in front of the room, and the tall kids sat in back, because they could see over the short kids' heads. I'm still the shortest kid in the class, so I'm in the front row, in an end seat, next to a boy named Spencer. Willa grew a little bit taller. She's also in the front row, but a little farther down. Her seat is in between Lucy and Clark.

Here are some of the other kids in our class:

Talisa
Arielle
Asher
Joshua
Maddie

Talisa is my second-best friend, and Arielle is my third-best friend. I'm not friends with Asher, but Willa is. She is friends with everyone except the meanies, like Joshua, who makes up mean names. Also once he pinched Talisa for no reason.

After our social studies lesson on Monday, Mrs. Finkel clapped her hands. That meant it was snack time.

There are two times we get to eat in school: at snack time and at lunch. Snack time is shorter and it comes first. At snack time we're allowed to stand up and stretch for five minutes. Then we have to go back to our desks and eat our snacks. Usually Mom packs

Joshua

me apple slices and a piece of candy, but that day I just had the apple.

I got up and walked over to Willa's desk, which is what I always do. I put my hands together and stretched my arms up over my head. Then I twisted my hands upside-down so my knuckles made a cracking sound. I've seen my dad do the same thing, but his knuckles crack louder than mine. My knuckles crack like the sound of pop rocks in your mouth, but Dad's crack like you're breaking apart a really thick bar of chocolate. It sounds like it hurts but really it doesn't.

"Is your mom coming here or meeting us at the store?" Willa asked. Mom was going to be one of the chaperones for the field trip to Batts Confections. We were going to have lunch and do a candy art project. I picked it out. Mom and Dad had given me a choice—

we could make a big candy mural, or we could decorate cookies. I decided on cookie decorating because that way each kid could bring something home.

"She's coming here," I told Willa. "She's going to ride on the bus with us."

Right then there was a knock on the classroom door and then it opened. I thought it would be Mrs. Bower. I knew she would say, "Are you coming to lunch today, Dara?" And then Mrs. Finkel would have to say "no," because she would be having lunch with us in the party room at the candy store.

But it wasn't Mrs. Bower at the door. It was a lady I had never seen before. She stepped into the room and went to talk to Mrs. Finkel. They whispered together in that way teachers do sometimes, so the kids can't hear. Then she looked up and waved. Clark waved back.

"Who's that?" Willa asked him.

"That's Mrs. Blank," Clark said. "She works in the learning lab."

Clark has to go to the learning lab for reading because he needs extra help. I feel bad for him about that. But he's really smart about other things. He can name all the presidents, and all the capitals.

"I've never seen her before," Willa said.

"She's new," Clark said.

"So she's like fill in the Mrs. Blank," Lucy said.

"What?" Clark asked.

"Blank is like nothing," Lucy said. "It's like she doesn't have a name and you have to fill it in."

"Oh, you mean like Mad Libs," Clark said.

"Yeah, just like that," Lucy said.

"That's not very nice," Willa said. "We shouldn't make fun of her name." Willa was right. That's the kind of thing Joshua would do.

"I wasn't making fun," Lucy said. "Anyway, it's okay because she didn't hear me."

Lucy is sometimes just the eensy weensiest bit of a meanie, but we're still friends with her. She's definitely not mean like Joshua is, and she's also very brave.

Mrs. Finkel clapped her hands together to let us know it was time to go back to our desks, so I went back to my desk and pulled out my snack.

CHAPTER 3

It's a Deal

I sat next to Willa on the bus over to Batts Confections. Mom sat next to Mr. Forman, who was the other chaperone. He's this girl, Maddie's, dad.

Batts Confections is in an outdoor shopping area. There are seven other stores right by it. Here are the other stores:

Long's Drugs
Safeway (that's a supermarket)

Brody's Grill

Man's Best Friend (that's a pet store)

Madden Stationery & Supplies

Kidz Cuts

A new store that's under construction right now, which Dad says is going to be a bookstore.

When the bus pulled up in front of Batts Confections, Mrs. Finkel stood up at the front and clapped her hands to get our attention. Then she told us the Ground Rules. We always have the same Ground Rules on every field trip: no disruptive behavior like running or yelling, no talking to strangers or taking anything that doesn't belong to you, and you have to stick with your buddy.

Willa was my buddy, like she always is. I stuck with her as we got off the bus and headed into the store.

The first thing you see when you walk into Batts Confections is the garden. It looks just like a real garden, but it's made of candy. There's ground-up chocolate for dirt, and flowers that are really lollypops. Little gummy worms peek out of the soil.

The very best part of the garden is the chocolate waterfall. Kids are allowed to dip marshmallows or Oreos or strawberries into it. You hold them out on a stick and they get covered in chocolate and taste so delicious. Dad says he's going to take out the garden as soon as he thinks of a really good idea of what to put in next. He says it's just about time for a change.

For the field trip, we had to go into the party room. We walked toward the back of the store, past the Stella's Fudge Counter and the Penny Candy Wall. That's the part of the store that's named after Penny, and each piece of candy costs just one cent.

Some of the people who work at Batts Confections called out, "Hi Stella, Hi Elaine." Elaine is my mom's name.

The party room was set up to look like a fancy dining room in a castle. The table is long and looks like it's made of really dark wood, but actually it's plastic because that's easier to clean. The chairs match the table, and there's a mural on the wall that looks like windows looking out onto a moat that is out front.

"Oh, look at that!" Joshua yelled. He was pointing to the glass case of the Crown Jewels, which are cookie crowns that have a special coating called shellacking on them so they don't go rotten, but then you can't eat them. They're decorated with rock candies that look like giant diamonds and rubies and emeralds, and they were really hard to make. That's why Dad keeps them in a glass case. People are allowed to look at them, but not touch them. Except one time, when the store was closed, Dad opened up the case and Penny and I got to try them on.

"I need to hear an indoor tone, Joshua," Mrs. Finkel said in her warning voice.

Joshua stepped closer to the case holding the Crown Jewels. "Too bad they aren't real," he said. He wasn't yelling, but he was still loud enough for most people to hear. "If they were, they'd cost a lot of money and Stella would be rich."

Just then I saw Stuart walk into the room. Dad calls Stuart a "kid." He's younger than Dad but he's not really a kid because he goes to college, and he works at Batts Confections to make money for his books and stuff. Stuart went over to say something to Mom.

"The pizza has arrived," Mom announced.

"Kids, take your seats," Mrs. Finkel said.

I sat with the same group I always sit with in the cafeteria at school. Willa, of course, and also Talisa, Arielle, and Lucy. Mom, Stuart,

Mr. Forman, and Mrs. Finkel came around and gave us slices of pizza. Willa got a special slice—with no tomato sauce, because she's allergic to tomatoes. Actually, she's allergic to a lot of things, like hazelnuts and blueberries and fish. I'm allergic to lettuce, but not really, I just don't like it.

"Knock knock," Talisa said.

"Who's there?" we all asked.

"Hurry up," she said.

"Hurry up who?"

"Hurry up and eat your pizza so we can get to dessert!"

Talisa is always telling knock-knock jokes. Sometimes, they don't make any sense. But we did try to eat fast, because after that we were going to do our sugary activity.

After we finished our pizza, we had to bring our garbage over to the big garbage can on the other side of the room. Dad had it painted gold so it would look like it belonged in a castle. Then we sat back down and the grownups passed out the sugar cookies. They weren't round, like regular cookies. There were kind of rectangular-shaped, so it was like a piece of paper you could draw a picture on. And they were bigger than regular cookies, like the size of two grown-up hands put together.

The cookie decorating supplies were set up in the middle of the table—frosting and paintbrushes so we could paint the frosting onto the cookies. There were a bunch of toppings we could stick onto the frosting, like jelly beans and M&Ms and Reese's Pieces and gumdrops.

"I think I'm going to make a landscape," Willa said.

"I'm going to make a rhinoceros," Talisa said. "Is there any gray icing?"

There was just about every color of icing except gray icing. "No," I said.

"What colors do you think would make gray if I mixed them together?" she asked.

"If you mixed all the colors together, I bet it would come out gray," I said. "That's what happens when Penny mixes all the paint colors together at home."

"Hey, look, is that Stella's Fudge?" Lucy asked, pointing to the little cubes of fudge in a bowl on the table next to the rainbow sprinkles.

Joshua had hopped up and was standing behind Talisa. "Duh, of course it is," he said.

"I wasn't talking to you," Lucy told him. "Go sit in your seat."

"I need to get some of the fudge cubes,"

Joshua said. "I'm building a model of my country house on my cookie." Joshua is the only kid in our class who has two houses—a regular house that he lives in every day, and a country house. He picked up the whole bowl of fudge.

"You can't take it all," Lucy told him.

"Why not?" Joshua asked. "You're not the fudge police."

"Yeah, but Stella is," Lucy said. "Tell him,

Stella. It's your fudge, after all. Tell him he can't have all the fudge."

"The fudge is for everyone to share," I said.

Joshua put the bowl back down, but then he reached in and scooped out a bunch of the pieces.

"You're taking them all," Lucy complained.

"No, I'm not," he said. "There are still

some left."

"Only two," Lucy said.

Joshua started to walk away and one of the pieces of fudge fell out of his hand and onto Talisa's cookie.

"Now look what you did," Lucy said. "It looks like there's a poop on her cookie. Like there's an elephant making poop."

"It's a rhinoceros," Talisa said. She picked up the fudge and popped it into her mouth.

"Ew, you just ate rhino poop," Joshua told her. "No wonder you're friends with Smella."

Everyone looked at me and I knew they were thinking about that time I don't even want to write about. Mrs. Finkel called out, "Joshua, take your seat," and I was glad he was in trouble.

I wished my name was a blank so I could just fill it in with whatever I wanted. That's

what parents should do when kids are born—
they should just leave their kids' names blank.
Then when the kids get old enough, they can
decide on their own names. There are a lot of
choices for names in the world, but you never
get to pick the one you want.

"Joshua is such a Poophead," Lucy said.

"Yeah," Talisa said. "That should be his
name."

"That's not nice," Willa said. "Two wrongs
don't make a right."

I thought Poophead was a good new
name for Joshua, but I didn't say anything.
Once Joshua said, "Willa gives me the willies,"
but Willa is never mean back.

"Do you guys want to know a secret?" I
asked.

"Tell us," Lucy said.

"You have to promise not to tell anyone,"

I said.

"I promise," Lucy said.

"Everyone has to promise," I said.

The other girls said they promised, too. Except Arielle just nodded, because she's always quiet. And Talisa didn't say she promised. She said, "Knock knock."

"Who's there?" I asked.

"Cross my heart," she said.

"Cross my heart who?"

"Cross my heart and hope to die, stick a needle in my eye," she said. The part about sticking a needle in her eye was really gross. It almost made my eyes start to hurt.

"Okay," I said. The girls leaned in and I lowered my voice so no one else could hear. "Here's the secret. I think I'm going to change my name so it's not Stella anymore," I said.

"Isn't that against the law?" Lucy asked.

"No," Talisa said. "Remember how Mrs. Gibson used to be Miss Porter?"

"That's because she got married. And that was her last name," Lucy pointed out.

"Maybe you just have to ask your parents first," Talisa said.

"I'm not going to tell my parents," I said. "Not until I decide on my new name."

"I thought you picked it out already," Willa said.

I shook my head. "I have to think about it. I don't want to get stuck with the wrong name again. I want to make sure I have a name with a nickname."

"What about Stella's Fudge?" Lucy asked.

"I guess they'll have to change that, too," I said.

"You know, I might change my name, too," Talisa said. "It's too weird."

"Me too," Willa said. Maybe she was remembering what Joshua had said.

"I like the name Reese," Lucy said.

"Ooh," Willa said. "Like Reese's Pieces and Reese's Peanut Butter Cups."

"You could all change your names," Arielle said.

Everyone turned to look at her. We always listen to what she says because usually she's quiet.

"Oh yeah," Talisa said. "We could all be different candies."

"I claim Reese," Lucy said.

I didn't mind that she claimed the name Reese because I didn't want that name anyway. It didn't have a nickname.

It was cool that my friends wanted to change their names, too. Imitation is the sincerest form of flattery. Having your friends imitate you is totally different than when your little sister does.

"Okay, this is the deal," I said. "We have to think about it and make sure we all pick the right names. Everyone should decide on a new name by tomorrow. And don't tell anyone else until then."

We all shook hands on it, even though our hands were sticky with candy. It took a little while because we had to make sure that each shook everyone else's hands. That meant it was a deal.

CHAPTER 4

Girls Named Caramel

Every day, we have a carpool after school: me, Penny, Willa, and Penny's friend Zoey. On Mondays, Mr. G usually picks us up. That's Willa's dad. The "G" stands for "Getter." My parents call Willa "Willa Go-Getter."

But this week the carpool schedule was all mixed up. Since my mom was the field-trip chaperone, she came back with us on the bus. Her car was in the parking lot at school and she told Mr. G she would drive us all home.

That meant Penny and I would get dropped off last. When other parents are driving, Penny and I get dropped off first, because our house is closest.

Mom's car has three rows of seats: the front seat, the back seat, and the way back. Everyone likes to sit in the way back because you get to face the other way. You can wave at people in other cars and sometimes they wave back. That day it was Willa's and my turn to have the way back, so Penny and Zoey had to sit in the regular back seat.

We got into the car and buckled up. Mom turned the radio on because she likes to have music when she's driving. Mom, Penny, and Zoey started singing along to a song called "Uh-oh." There's a part of the song where you're supposed to snap. Mom never snaps when she's driving because she has to keep her hands on the wheel. Penny doesn't know how to snap so she claps instead.

"I know what my new name is going to be," Willa said as we pulled out of the parking lot.

I put my finger to my lips, like the school librarian does when we're getting too noisy. "Shh," I told her.

"It's okay," Willa said. "Penny and Zoey aren't listening, and your mom's up front so

she can't hear."

"You should still whisper, just in case," I said.

"I'm going to be Caramel," Willa said. Even though she was whispering I could tell she was excited.

"Caramel Getter," Willa said. "Cara for short. Doesn't it sound great?"

It did sound great. It sounded better than great. It was just about the best name in the whole world.

Why didn't I think of the name Caramel first? I love caramel. I mean, I really LOVE it. It's one of my favorite kinds of candy. They sell caramel at Batts Confections, and sometimes Mom puts a couple of pieces in my lunchbox. I have a special way of eating them. I suck on them instead of chewing them, because then they last longer. When we go out for ice cream, Penny always asks for chocolate sauce on top, but I pick caramel. There's even a caramel flavor kind of Stella's Fudge.

I'd forgotten all about caramel, but it really was the perfect name for me: Caramel Batts. Cara Batts. Or even Carrie Batts. It was such a great name that it had *two* nicknames!

"It sounds really cool," I said. "I think I'll make that my name too."

"You can't be Caramel if I'm already Caramel," Willa said.

"Why not? Imitation is the sincerest form of flattery."

"I don't know what you mean," Willa said.

"I mean we could be Caramel B and

Caramel G," I said. "Just like Haley H and Haley V."

"It's still confusing when there are two," Willa said. "Remember that time when we meant to have a play date with Haley V and my mom called Haley H's mom by mistake?"

I did remember. Haley H started to cry when she found out she was invited by mistake. It's definitely easier when everyone has their own name. But then Mrs. G said Haley V and Haley H should both come over, and we had a really good time.

Changing my name had been my idea first, so I thought I should probably get to make the rules. But if I told Willa that, she'd think I was just being a meanie.

"We're not supposed to decide on our names until tomorrow," I reminded her.

"We can decide whenever we want. We

just have to tell everyone tomorrow," Willa said.

"But if you decide too fast you could pick the wrong name," I told her.

"No, I love it," Willa said. "You're just saying that because you want to be Caramel."

"No I'm not," I said, even though that was sort of a lie.

"I can help you think of another name," Willa said. "There are lots of other good candy names. What about Taffy, like saltwater taffy."

"I don't really like taffy," I said.

"What about Clark? You know, like a Clark Bar?"

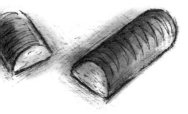 "Clark is a boy's name," I reminded her. "Like Clark

in our class. Besides, those names don't have good nicknames."

I tried to make a list of candy names in my head, but nothing sounded right. Bonbons, Licorice, Sweet Tarts, Starburst, Butterscotch. I mean, who wants to be called Butterscotch? What if I never found the right name? Or worse, what if there's a name that's meant for me, and I never get to have it?

Willa waved to the driver in the car behind us. It was a stranger, and sometimes it's fun to see if strangers will wave back. But then Mom turned the corner onto Lakeview Way, Willa's street, and the car that was behind us zoomed past. We pulled up in front of Willa's house. "Here you are, Willa Go-Getter," Mom said.

She honked the horn so Willa's mom would know to come outside.

Willa undid her seatbelt and climbed over the back seat. "Bye Stel," she said.

"Bye Willa."

She shook her head.

"From now on, my name is Caramel or Cara," she reminded me.

CHAPTER 5

Baby Girl Batts

That night Mom said, "I was so busy with Stella's class today, I forgot to bring the order binder home. I'm going to head back to the store to pick it up."

"I can go for you, Laney," Dad said.

I asked Dad if I could go with him and he said yes. My hair was wet because I had taken a bath. Usually I take a bath and just hang out at home until it's time to go to bed.

It was the first time I was riding in a car

with wet hair and pajamas, and it felt kind of funny. Well, I was only sort of in my pajamas. I had changed out of pajama pants into jeans, but I kept my pajama top on. It looked like a regular long-sleeved shirt so I don't think anyone could tell.

Dad opened the door to the store and there was that special aroma (aroma is another word for smell) that just means Batts Confections. It's a mix of chocolate and mint and cinnamon and a million different other candy flavors. I wish I could wrap it around myself, like a blanket. It's so comfy.

We walked inside and I looked over at the Stella's Fudge Counter. There were two customers taste-testing different fudge flavors. I could tell they were taste-testing because Stuart was giving them eensy weensy pieces. Mom calls them "slivers." People can have slivers of as many different flavors as they want. That way they can decide what their favorite is, and then they can buy it.

When Stuart saw Dad and me he waved. "Well if it isn't Miss Stella," he said. "How lucky am I to see Stella Batts twice in one day! Hello Stella!"

I got a funny feeling when Stuart said my name over and over like that. It almost didn't sound like my name anymore, and it made me feel shy.

"Hey darling, do you want to stay up here or do you want to come down to the office with me?" Dad asked.

"I want to go with you," I told him.

We said goodbye to Stuart and then we walked through the door marked "PRIVATE" that's behind the cash registers. I love going through that door because regular people

aren't allowed.

Behind the "PRIVATE" door, there's a small hallway that leads to a staircase. There's also an elevator. Dad says it's a freight elevator, which means it's there to move boxes from

one floor to another, and not really for people.

Mom and Dad share an office in the basement. To get to it, they usually walk down the stairs. When I'm with Dad, we get to take the elevator so I can press the buttons. (Mom won't ever take the elevator—not even when I'm with her—because one time she got stuck in an elevator and now she's afraid of them.)

I pressed the button for the elevator and the doors opened. We stepped inside and I pressed the button marked "C," which stands for cellar. That's another word for basement.

The elevator is pretty slow, so it's lucky we only had to go down one floor. Dad pulled a ring of keys out of his pocket and unlocked the office door. He flipped on the light switch and walked over to his desk. Then he cracked his knuckles. "If I were the order binder, where would I be?" he said. I knew he was talking to himself and not me, because he does that sometimes.

As he looked around, he started piling up other things—a box of samples from a new candy supply company, some papers and catalogues, and a green shopping bag, which was the same shade of green as the green kind of M&Ms. It was tied with a white satin ribbon, which made it look kind of like a present.

"I thought you just needed to get Mom's binder," I said.

"I did," Dad said. "But whenever I'm in here I find other things I could work on."

"Oh," I said. "What's in the bag?" I noticed a label on the side, with SCHEHERAZADE written in fancy letters.

"It's from Fran, who runs the new bookstore. It's just about set to open and your mom sent over a basket of chocolate-covered pretzels as a 'Welcome-to-the-Neighborhood' gift, so Fran dropped this off to thank her."

"What is it?" I asked.

"I imagine it's a book," Dad said.

"Is the bookstore called Scher—I can't say that word."

"It's pronounced SHUH-HARA-ZA-DUH," Dad said. "It means a woman who's a good storyteller."

"Cool," I said. I didn't know there was a word for that. I said it in my head slowly, the way Dad had. It was five syllables, which was one more than Penelope. It sounded really fancy.

"Oh, there you are," he said, suddenly

talking to the order binder. It had been right smack in the middle of his desk the whole time. He put the binder on top of the pile and picked up the whole thing. "It's always the last place you look."

"But it has to be the last place you look, because once you find something, you stop looking," I told him.

"You're too smart for me," Dad said.

"I can help you carry some things if you want," I said.

"Thank you, darling." He handed me the bag to hold and carried the rest himself.

"You always call me 'darling,'" I said. Dad locked the office up again and we headed toward the elevator.

"That's because you're my darling," Dad said.

I pressed the button and the elevator door

opened. We stepped inside and I pressed the button marked "1." "How did you decide on the name Stella?" I asked.

"You know this story," Dad said.

"I want to hear it again," I said. That's another one of my favorite things—hearing stories about when I was little. I forgot to put it on my list.

"Okay, darling," he said. The elevator door opened right then and I followed Dad back into the store.

Stuart called out, "Hey Stel, come here."

Dad pushed me toward the fudge counter, so I had to go. Stuart held out a fudge sliver. "It's our newest flavor," he said. "Peanut butter cookie dough fudge."

I looked over at Dad. I had already had dessert with dinner, so I wasn't sure if I was allowed to taste it, even though it was just an eensy weensy piece.

"Go ahead," Dad said.

I popped the fudge into my mouth and sucked on it, like it was a piece of caramel. I could taste all the flavors mixing together. The peanut butter and cookie dough and chocolate made the most perfect combination.

"Well?" Dad asked.

"I love it," I said.

"Say thank you to Stuart," he told me, even though I was going to say it on my own.

"Thanks," I said.

"I'm glad you liked it," Stuart said. "It's

the first flavor I invented, so thank you for trying it."

"You're welcome," I said.

I said it really softly, so Stuart said, "What?"

"You're welcome," I said a little more loudly. I don't know why I felt shy again, but I did. I reached for Dad's hand, even though that's kind of a babyish thing to do.

"Goodnight all," Dad said. "Our compliments to the chef."

"Bye Dave," Stuart said. Dave is my dad's name—short for David. He has a nickname, too.

We got to the car and Dad put all of his stuff next to me in the back seat. He waited for me to put on my seatbelt and then he turned the key to start the engine.

"You forgot to tell me the name story," I

said.

"I'll tell you now," Dad said. "Mommy was pregnant with you. We were so excited because we were about to have our very first baby. We didn't know if you would be a boy or a girl, so we had two names picked out."

"Nicole for a girl and Andrew for a boy," I said.

"Exactly right," Dad said. "But then you were born and the nurse asked us for a name for the birth certificate. Mom and I looked at you and we both thought the same thing."

"You didn't think I looked like a Nicole."

"Nope," Dad said. "And of course you didn't look like an Andrew, either, but those were the only two names we had agreed on. So the nurse just put 'Baby Batts' on the little nametag around your ankle. Mom and I called you 'BB' for short."

"I had a nickname back then," I said.

"You did," Dad said. "But we still had to come up with a name to put on your birth certificate. Some other parents had left behind a baby-name book. The nurse gave it to us, and Mom and I started reading the names out loud to you, to see what would fit. You know, it's a big decision to name someone. Your kid will have to live with that decision for the rest of her life."

"The rest of someone's life is a long time," I said.

"It sure is," Dad said. "Then, at one point, I was trying to get you to fall asleep and I was reading the name book to you. I said, 'Sweet dreams, little Stella.'"

"And I closed my eyes."

"Yes, exactly," Dad said. "You seemed to know I was talking to you. I looked over at

Mommy and asked her what she thought of the name Stella. She loved it as much as I did, so that became your name."

"Did you ever think you made a mistake?" I asked. "Like maybe it sounded like an old lady's name, or maybe I wouldn't like it?"

"Nope, not for one second," Dad said. "It's who you are. Now it's my favorite name."

"More favorite than the name Penelope?"

"They're both my favorite names," Dad said. "My favorite names for my favorite girls."

He clicked the rearview mirror down so he could see me in the back seat, and then he smiled at me. It made me feel kind of bad about not liking my name. But I couldn't help it.

Just then Dad drove over a bump and the stuff in the back seat slid over toward me. The bag from Fran fell into my lap. I twirled the satin ribbon around my fingers. It felt so soft, like fresh fudge, or actually even softer. It was almost squishy, like a giraffe's lips. Most people don't know what giraffe lips feel like, but I touched a giraffe at the zoo last year. It bent its long neck down and its lips brushed against my hand. I was scared at first, but it didn't hurt me at all. It was very gentle.

I turned the bag over so I could see the label again: Scheherazade. I let go of the ribbon and traced the letters so I could remember how to spell it. Scheherazade.

Scheherazade. Scheherazade. It was a name for a writer. Maybe it could be my new name. My life would probably be totally different with a name like that. I could be Scheherazade, a really good storyteller, who wouldn't ever slip and fall. People could call me Sherry for short. They would never, ever call me Smella.

And my new name would look perfect on the cover of my book.

CHAPTER 6

New Names

The next day, we had a safety expert talk to us at snack time, which meant we didn't get to tell each other our new names until lunch. The five of us sat together, the way we always do. As soon as we got to our table, Lucy said, "You guys, I have the best new name!"

"Me too," Talisa said.

"Me three," Willa and I said at the same time.

"Jinx!" Lucy said, so Willa and I couldn't

talk until someone said our names backwards.

"Jinx shouldn't count this time because you don't even know their new names," Talisa said.

"Fine," Lucy said. "But then I get to say my new name first."

I thought I should get to go first, because it was my idea. But I didn't say anything.

"Isn't Reese your new name?" Willa asked, since now she was allowed to speak. "Nope, I thought of a better one," Lucy said. "Try and guess it."

"Um, I don't know," Willa said. "Skittle?"

"No, that's not a name."

"How about Joy, like an Almond Joy," Talisa said.

"Wrong again," Lucy said. "Arielle and Stella, you should try and guess too."

Arielle shook her head. "I can't think of

any. You still look like a Lucy to me."

"Is it Sara?" I asked.

"No, silly, that's not the name of a candy," Lucy said.

"This is going to take a really long time," I said. "You should just say it."

"Truffle," Lucy said.

"That's not a name either," I said.

"It is now," Lucy said.

"Aren't truffles made from pig snouts?" Willa asked.

"Oh, gross," Talisa said.

"We have chocolate truffles in our store," I said. "They're made of fudge and things like nougat and toffee and marshmallow."

"That's exactly the kind of truffle I am,"

Lucy said. "A chocolate truffle. So that's what you should call me."

"We should call you 'Chocolate Truffle'?" Talisa asked. "It's kind of a long name."

"No, I mean just call me Truffle," Lucy said.

"What's your nickname?" Willa asked.

"I don't have one," Lucy said. "It's just 'Truffle,' but I don't care about having a nickname."

"Knock knock," Talisa said.

"Who's there?" we all asked.

"Kit," she said.

"Kit who?"

"Kit Kat," Talisa said.

"That's my new name. Isn't it great? Kit Kats are one of my favorite candies and 'Kit' can be my nickname."

"My new name is Caramel," Willa said. "You can call me Cara for short."

"Oh, that's so cool," Talisa said. "You're like me—your nickname is like a real name."

So it was just Arielle and me who hadn't said our new names yet. I had wanted to be the first, and now I was almost last.

"I'm Scheherazade," I said quickly, or as quickly as you can say that name. Then I felt like kind of a meanie for blurting it out, which meant Arielle would go last, even though everyone else had just been saying their names, too.

"Hairy what?" Lucy asked.

"SHUH-HARA-ZA-DUH," I said slowly, the way Dad had. "It means a woman who's good at telling stories."

"So it's not a candy?" Lucy asked. I knew I was supposed to call her Truffle, but I wasn't used to it yet. It was still easier to think of her as just plain Lucy.

"Nope," I said. "I couldn't think of a good candy name for me. It's the name of the new store in the shopping area where Batts

Confections is. You can call me Sherry for short."

"You have to have a candy name," Lucy said. "That's the deal we made."

"No it isn't," I said. "We just made a deal to pick new names."

"How about Sherbet?" Lucy asked. "We could still call you Sherry for short."

"Sherbet's like ice cream," I said. "It's not a candy. Besides, I don't like that name." It was only two syllables, which was the same as my old name.

"I think Stella—I mean Sherry—should get to have whatever name she wants," Willa said.

"Hey, you'll get to have the same initials," Talisa said. "S.B."

"So Arielle, what's your new name?" Lucy asked.

"I don't have one," she said.

"We can help you think of one," Talisa offered.

"Yeah, you could be Reese, since I'm not Reese anymore," Lucy said.

Arielle shook her head and said something so softly I couldn't even hear. "What?" I asked.

"I like my name," Arielle said.

"But yesterday you said you didn't," Lucy said.

"I just said you guys could change your names," Arielle said. "I didn't say I wanted to change mine."

"That's okay," Willa said. "You don't have to."

I thought Arielle was

a pretty name. Sometimes we call her Ari, which is a good nickname. But I bet if what happened to me happened to Arielle, Joshua would call her "Arismell," and then she'd probably want to change her name, too.

"When do we tell everyone our new names?" Talisa asked.

"We should just make an announcement," Lucy said.

"But Miss Linka isn't here," Willa said. "We have Mr. Moyers, and he probably won't let us."

Miss Linka is nicest of all the lunch aides. She doesn't yell at kids if they accidentally spill something, and she lets us trade desserts. But she'd told us on Friday that she would be out all week, and Mr. Moyers would be subbing.

Mr. Moyers was the lunch aide from last year, and he's the opposite of Miss Linka. He makes everybody stay at their tables during lunch, and he only lets two kids go to the bathroom at a time. He's old so he retired, and he just fills in sometimes when Miss Linka is absent. It didn't really matter on Monday, since we had lunch at the candy store. But now that we were back in the lunchroom, he was in charge

and he was a total meanie.

"I'll ask him," Lucy said. "I'm not afraid of him."

"Yeah, but then he might get mad at all of us," Talisa pointed out.

"We could do it at recess," Willa said. Recess is right after lunch. We have a half hour to hang out in the yard, and then we have to go back to class.

"Everyone will be running around and not paying attention," Lucy said.

"How about if we ask Mrs. Finkel if we can make a class announcement?" Willa suggested.

So that was what we decided to do.

CHAPTER 7

The Announcement

The thing that Lucy did in class is the craziest thing I've ever had to write about. It started because Mrs. Finkel wouldn't let us make an announcement during class time about our new names.

"But last month you let Henry make an announcement during class time," Lucy reminded her. Henry is another boy in our class.

"That   was   a   different   kind   of

announcement," Mrs. Finkel said. "Remember Henry was running a canned-food drive for needy kids. It was for a very good cause."

"This is a good cause," Lucy said. "We need new names."

"You all have very nice names," Mrs. Finkel said.

"I knew you were going to say that," Lucy said. "You have to say that."

"It's normal for kids to be unhappy with their names," Mrs. Finkel said. "When I was young, I didn't like mine either. But I'm sure one day you'll start to like your names, and then you might feel bad about changing them."

"We might not," I said.

"That's true," Mrs. Finkel said. "But I still can't let you make an announcement about your names during class time. I'm supposed to call you by the names I have in my marking book. Now take your seats, because it's time for math."

We turned to head back to our desks. Mrs. Finkel started clapping her hands to get everyone's attention. "Don't worry, Sherry," Lucy whispered to me. "I have a plan."

When I got to my desk, I clicked my heels together three times, like Dorothy in *The Wizard of Oz*. Even though I didn't know what Lucy's plan was, I wished that it would work.

Part of third-grade math is to learn about money. Everyone already knows how much different coins are worth, but Mrs. Finkel makes us do all kinds of math problems with them. She says it's important to know how to pay for things. Like if you go into a store and something costs 45 cents, you should know what different combinations of coins you can use. And if you pay with a dollar, you should know how much change to get back, just in case the cashier makes a mistake. It's easy for me because I've helped out with the cash register at Batts Confections. When someone buys a Batts Bar for 85 cents and pays with

a dollar, I know all the ways to give them 15 cents back.

"All right," Mrs. Finkel said, "if something costs seventy-seven cents, what's the least amount of coins you can use to pay for it?"

A bunch of people raised their hands. I knew the answer, but I didn't raise my hand. Willa and Lucy both did. Joshua raised his hand and waved it around. He likes everything that has to do with money. He's always talking about how much things cost, and how his parents give him all the money he wants. Lucy says if he's so rich, he should live in a mansion. We all know his house isn't a mansion because in first grade his mom was the class parent and the end-of-the-year party was at his house. But he does have two houses, so I still think he's rich.

Mrs. Finkel won't call on you if you wave your hand around. She says that's disruptive behavior, and all you have to do is raise your hand calmly. She called on Maddie, who was raising her hand straight up in the air.

"Four," Maddie said. "A fifty-cent coin, a quarter and two pennies."

"Wrong!" Joshua called out. "There's no such thing as a fifty-cent coin."

"Joshua," Mrs. Finkel said in her warning voice.

"Sorry," he said. "But there isn't."

"Actually there is," she told him. "But

most people don't use it. Good job, Maddie. That was a trick question and you got it. Now can you tell me how many coins if you didn't have the fifty-cent piece?"

"Five," Maddie said. "Three quarters and two pennies."

"Exactly right," Mrs. Finkel said. "Can anyone else tell me the most amount of coins you can use?"

Five kids raised their hands again, including Joshua. He didn't wave it around, but you could tell that he really wanted to.

"Okay, Joshua," Mrs. Finkel said.

"Seven dimes and

seven pennies," he said.

"No, not quite," Mrs. Finkel said.

Joshua slammed his hand on the desk. That's what he always does when he's upset or when he gets the answer wrong.

"It's all right, Joshua," Mrs. Finkel said. "It's okay to have the wrong answer sometimes, as long as you try your best. But no more disruptive behavior, or I'm going to have to send you to Mr. O'Neil to calm down." Mr. O'Neil is our principal.

"Anyone else?" Mrs. Finkel asked.

Lucy raised her hand. "Yes, Lucy," Mrs. Finkel said.

"First of all, my name isn't Lucy anymore. It's Truffle. Willa is Caramel, Talisa is Kit Kat, and Stella is Scher—just Sherry. We're all named after candies, except for Sherry," Lucy said. She was talking really quickly. "And the answer is seventy-seven pennies."

"That's enough, Lucy. We discussed this," Mrs. Finkel said. She sounded really mad. My cheeks felt hot so I knew I was blushing. But it was exciting too. Now everyone knew our names.

CHAPTER 8

Sherry & Stella

Mrs. Finkel said Lucy's announcement counted as disruptive behavior and we weren't allowed to make any more announcements without permission, or else we'd be sent to Mr. O'Neil. I didn't think it was exactly fair that Willa, Talisa, and I got in trouble, too—since Lucy was the one who made the announcement. For the rest of the day, I tried to be extra good in class.

After school, Zoey's mom, Mrs. Benson,

drove the carpool home. Mrs. Benson's car has a back seat and a way back too, but the way back doesn't face backwards so we don't have to take turns. Willa and I always sit in the back seat, and Penny and Zoey always sit in the way back.

We all got into the car. Penny and Zoey got in first, and then Willa and me—Willa, who was now Caramel. Mrs. Benson made sure we were all buckled up before she started the car. "Hey, Sherry," Willa said.

Penny leaned forward. "Who are you talking to?" she asked.

"Your sister," Willa said. "Her name isn't Stella anymore. She changed it to Sherry."

"Willa, don't," I said. "Oops, I mean Cara."

"Don't be mad. I thought it would be okay to say, since we made an announcement," Willa said. I mean Cara said. I'm still used to her old name.

"You changed your name too?" Zoey asked.

"Yup," Willa said.

"Stella and Willa changed their names," Penny said loudly.

"Like the Artist Formerly Known as Prince," Mrs. Benson said.

I knew the word "formerly" meant something that used to be, but I was still confused. "What do you mean?" I asked.

"When I was younger, there was a singer named Prince who was very popular. Then one day he decided to change his name, and people started calling him 'The Artist Formerly Known as Prince,'" Mrs. Benson explained.

"You don't have to call me 'The Girl Formerly Known as Willa,'" Willa said. "You can just call me Caramel, or Cara for short. And Sherry is a nickname for . . . how do you say your whole name?"

"Scheherazade," I said.

"That's a mouthful," Mrs. Benson said.

"That's why you call her Sherry for short," Willa said.

"Okay, Cara and Sherry," Mrs. Benson said. "It's a pleasure to meet you."

"We're not new people," I said. "We just have new names."

"You certainly picked unique ones," Mrs. Benson said.

"What does unique mean?" Penny asked.

"It's another word for unusual," I said.

"That's exactly right," Mrs. Benson said.

"Like the name Doodle is a unique name," Willa added.

Last year there was a girl in our class

named Doodle. At Willa's birthday party, Willa's mom told her, "You must be the first person named Doodle I've ever met." This year Doodle's in Mrs. Bower's class, so we don't see her as much.

Just then we pulled up in front of our house. Mrs. Benson honked the horn and Mom came to the front door. Penny and I climbed out of the car and walked up the sidewalk. "Hey Mom!" Penny called. "Guess what? You'll never guess what!"

"What?" Mom asked. She waved to everyone in Mrs. Benson's car and closed the door behind Penny and me.

"Stella and Willa changed their names!" Penny said.

"Oh, really?" Mom asked. "What are their names now?"

Penny started to say, but I interrupted

her. It was my new name, so I should get to tell. "I'm Sherry," I said.

"It's short for something," Penny said.

"Scheherazade," I said. "Like the new bookstore."

"You're right, I never would've guessed that," Mom said.

"And Willa's new name is Caramel, but you can call her Cara," Penny added.

"What made you change your names?" Mom asked. "Are you playing a name game?"

"No, it's not a game," I said. "We just didn't like our names that much, so we decided to change them."

"But I love the name Stella," Mom said.

"Mom, I need a snack," Penny said. Penny and I always like to have snacks after we get home from school.

"What do you say?" Mom asked.

"Please," Penny said, and she turned to head toward the kitchen.

"Wait, your shoes," Mom said. My parents have this rule that we have to take our shoes off before we walk around the house, so we don't bring germs inside. Sometimes it's hard to remember even though it's been the rule for my whole life.

We kicked off our shoes and lined them up by the door, because that's what we're supposed to do. Then we went to the kitchen and sat down in our seats. Mom put a bowl of grapes in the middle of the table. It's funny how Mom gives us mostly healthy snacks when she works all

day in a confections store and we could have all the candy we want.

Mom poured milk for Penny and me, and stuck straws in the glasses because that's how we like to drink them. "Thanks," I said. "Thanks," Penny said right after me. If she had said it at the exact same time, I would've said jinx.

"You're welcome," Mom said. She sat down in her seat, which is next to mine. Dad's seat is across from Mom's, next to Penny's.

You can blow the best bubbles in milk—much better than water or juice. Mom says it's fine for Penny and me to blow bubbles in our drinks. But if we make a mess, then we have to clean it up ourselves. I started blowing little bubbles in my milk. I like to watch them climb up the sides of the glass.

"I'm sad you don't like your name, Stel," Mom said.

"You mean Sherry," Penny said.

"Stella's not a good name," I said. "It

doesn't have a nickname, except for . . . except for Smella."

"Who calls you that?" Mom asked.

"Joshua in my class said it," I said.

"When?"

"The first time was last week."

"When you fell?" Mom asked. I nodded. Mom knew about what happened because Mrs. Tucker—that's the school nurse—called her and told her to bring me new pants. Mine were all ruined.

"I don't want to talk about it," I told her.

Just then the phone rang. Mom reached over and checked the little caller ID screen to see who was calling. She pressed the "talk" button and said, "Hey, honey."

"Hi, Daddy!" Penny shouted toward the phone. She knew it had be to Dad, because he and Penny and I are the only ones Mom calls "honey," and Penny and I were right there at the table with her.

"Daddy says hi," Mom told her.

"Stella changed her name!" Penny said.

Dad must've asked Mom about it, because then Mom said, "She did, because one of the boys in her class has been giving her a hard time since she fell and landed in that dog mess last week."

I wished she would stop talking about it. I told her I didn't want to talk about it, which meant I didn't want to hear about it either. I hated even thinking about it, because when I thought about it, I remembered everything. We were walking in the woods behind our school. Mrs. Finkel said the kids in the back had to hurry up. Lucy and Willa started to run and I followed them, and then I tripped. Joshua saw the whole thing. "Ew, there's dog

poop all over Stella!" he told everyone. "Ew, it stinks. I think her new name is Smella." Everyone laughed—especially the boys. Boys always laugh at things like that. I tried really hard not to cry but I couldn't help it, because it actually hurt a lot where I fell. Mrs. Finkel came over and said we had to cut the nature walk short so she could take me to the nurse's office. Then Joshua said, "Oh, man," and looked at me like I'd ruined everything.

Mom talked to Dad for a few more

minutes, mostly about some stuff for the store. I blew bubbles in my milk. Sometimes I like to see how I can make the bubbles different sizes depending on how hard I blow—like little ones the size of runts, and big ones the size of gobstopper sucking candies. But right then I wasn't really in the mood.

Mom hung up the phone and turned to me. "When I was a kid, someone once said, 'Here comes Hurricane Elaine.' I was afraid everyone would think I was messy, so I thought about changing my name," she said. "But your name is who you are."

"I think it's cool to change your name," Penny said. "I want to change mine, too."

"Both my girls are changing their names now?" Mom asked. She rested her cup on her stomach. Having a baby inside you is like having a built-in shelf.

"Can you help me make a list of names, Sherry?" Penny asked.

"Sure," I said. "Mom, can we have paper?"

"You know where it is," Mom said. I stood up and ripped a sheet of paper off the message pad. I brought it back to the table along with a pencil.

"I'm ready," I said. "Name some names."

"Name some names. That's so funny," Penny said. "Sherry, Caramel, Zoey."

I held the pencil to the paper, but I didn't write anything down. "You already know people with those names," I told her. "Name some new names."

"How about Stella?" Penny said.

"You can't be Stella," I said. "It's my name."

"But you changed your name," Penny said. "I don't care if someone calls me Smella. I smell good, like the candy-apple shampoo. And it's not fair for you to get both Stella and Sherry. I want to have one of those names."

"She always copies me," I complained.

"Imitation is the sincerest form of flattery," Mom reminded me. "At least one of my daughters is keeping a name that I picked out."

"So does that mean I get to be Stella?" Penny asked.

I shrugged. "I guess so," I said. Mom patted my head, and I put the pencil down.

"Cool," Penny said. "That's what I've always wanted to be."

CHAPTER 9

Problems

The next day, we stood by Lucy's desk during snack time, talking about new names. Other kids wanted to change their names, too. Maddie said she would be Candace, since Candy was a good nickname for Candace. And Asher said he would be Mike, like Mike and Ike candies. Even Joshua wanted to change his name. He said he wanted to be Richard.

"You can't change your name to Richard because it's not a candy," Lucy told him.

"So what?" he said. "Sherry isn't a candy either."

"It could be short for Sherbet," I said, even though that wasn't my name. I just didn't want Joshua to get the name he wanted, because he was always so mean to us—except that he hadn't called me Smella since I'd changed my name.

"That's right," Lucy said. "And sherbet is practically a candy."

"I don't care," Joshua said. "From now on, I'm Richard."

"He probably only wants to be Richard because it has the word 'rich' in it," Lucy told the rest of us.

Clark was sitting at his desk, two seats down, on the other side of Willa. "Can I change my name too?" he asked.

"Sure you can," Willa said.

"But your name is already a candy," Lucy pointed out. "You know, like a Clark Bar."

"Actually I really like the name Zach," Clark said.

"I know that name!" Talisa said. "My mom's friend just had a baby named Zach. They live in Florida."

"Sherry and I are going to Florida to swim with dolphins," Willa said.

Once on this show we love, *Superstar Sam,* the main girl named Sam and her friends went to a place in Florida called The Dolphin Sanctuary. They got into the water with the dolphins and held onto their fins. Then the dolphins started swimming fast and pulled the kids along.

Willa and I decided one day we would go there, too. It wasn't right for her to talk about going without me. She knows how much I love dolphins. It was strange, because she's not a meanie.

"But I thought I was going to go to Florida with you," I said.

"You ARE coming with me. YOU'RE Sherry," Willa reminded me.

"How could you forget your new name when it was your idea?" Talisa asked.

"I thought it was Truffle's idea," Clark said.

"Nope, it was Sherry's," Willa said.

"But I made the announcement," Lucy reminded everyone.

Then Mrs. Finkel clapped her hands, so we had to go back to our desks.

It was raining outside that day, which

meant that after lunch we had indoor recess. Indoor recess is when we stay in the lunchroom and play games. There are all sorts of board games, or you can play tag or Red Rover or Red Light Green Light. Usually I don't mind it, but I hate when Mr. Moyers is in charge. He walks up and down the room and yells if anyone gets too loud, even though it's recess and we're *supposed* to be loud.

Willa, Lucy, and I decided to have a Spit tournament. I don't mean spit like saliva. I mean Spit the card game. It works best when there are two players, because you each get half the cards. Once we tried to play with two decks of cards and four people, but it was too hard to keep track of everything. So Willa and Lucy would play first. Then I would play whoever won. The final winner would get to be champion of the tournament.

Willa counted out the cards for her and Lucy. I pulled out my notebook. As long as I was waiting for my turn, I could work on my book.

"What's that?" Lucy asked.

"It's my autobiography," I told her.

"Your what?"

"My book I'm writing that's about me."

I flipped it open and Lucy leaned over my shoulder. "Hey, you wrote Lucy," she said.

"I was writing a part that you were in," I said. "Don't worry, I didn't write anything bad."

"But my name is Truffle!" she said.

"I know that," I said. "It's just easier when I'm writing to use people's old names."

"That's not allowed," she said. She pulled my notebook from my hands. "Give me an eraser. I'm going to correct all the parts where you wrote the wrong names."

"No, you can't!" I said. "It's my book!"

"But you put my name in it," Lucy said.

"It's still mine! I'm allowed to write what I want!"

Just then Mr. Moyers walked up the aisle. He stopped at our table and stared down at me, his arms folded across his chest. His eyes are sort of too small for his face, like the size of Goobers. "What's the problem here, Miss Batts?"

"Nothing," I said.

"Nothing?" he repeated. "Is that why I could hear you screaming from across the room?"

"I wasn't screaming," I said. And it was true—I hadn't been screaming at all. I had just raised my voice the littlest eensy weensy bit, and only because Lucy took my notebook.

Mr. Moyers pulled the notebook from Lucy's hands. "Whose book is this?" he asked.

I was afraid to say it was mine, but Lucy is never afraid. She said, "I was just borrowing it. It's hers," and she pointed to me.

Mr. Moyers flipped open the front cover. Right then I wanted to scream for real. I wanted to say, "That's MY BOOK! Give it back RIGHT NOW!" What if he kept it forever and never gave it back? I had been working so hard on it. It wasn't fair. I thought about clicking my heels together to make a wish, but

I was afraid he'd see me and get even madder. I looked at my book in his hands. A couple of the pages were crumpled from when Lucy pulled it away. I wanted to hold my book and smooth the pages out, even though you can't unbend paper.

"I'm going to hold onto this until the end of recess," Mr. Moyers said, glaring at me with his mean little goober eyes. "Miss Batts, if you and your friends manage to keep your voices down for the rest of the period, then you can have it back."

He walked away to go yell at some other kids. Lucy didn't even say she was sorry. "Let's just play Spit," Willa said. "Sherry plays the winner."

"She shouldn't get to be Sherry if she keeps writing our old names," Lucy said. "Besides, she picked a name that's not a candy, and no one even knows how to say it."

"She'll practice the new names, right Sherry?" Willa asked.

"I can't practice without my notebook," I said.

"You'll get it back at the end of recess," Willa said. "We'll be extra quiet to make sure, right Truffle?"

"Okay," Lucy said. "But I'm not going to call you Sherry until you stop writing Lucy, because that's not my name anymore."

I nodded. I just wanted my notebook back, even though I wasn't in the mood to write anymore.

CHAPTER 10

My Very Own Name

I did get my book back at the end of recess. I decided never to bring it to school with me again. Actually, I didn't ever want to go to school again. At least not until Mr. Moyers was gone and I could remember everyone's new names. I made a list to keep track:

Stella—Scheherazade
Willa—Caramel
Talisa—Kit Kat

Lucy—Truffle
Asher—Mike
Maddie—Candace
Clark—Zach
Joshua—Richard

"Stella, it's bath time!" Mom called.

"I'm coming," I called back. I was just putting my pencil down when Penny came into my room.

"You're supposed to knock," I reminded her. It was probably about the millionth time I had told her the exact same thing.

"The door was partway open so I didn't think I had to knock," she said.

"Well I'm leaving my room anyway," I told her. "Mom just called me."

"That's what I came to tell you," Penny said. "Mom said 'Stella, it's bath time.' But *I'm*

Stella, remember? I told Mom she had to call me Stella from now on."

"I changed my mind," I told her. "You can't be Stella. It's too confusing if you're Stella."

"Why?" Penny asked. "It's not your name anymore. You're Sherry, remember?"

"Stella!" Mom called again.

"Coming!" Penny and I yelled at the same time.

"Jinx!" I said, and then Penny and I both ran down the hall, like we were racing, even though no one had said, "On your mark, get set, go!" Penny had a little head start because she'd been closer to the door when we started running. But I'm older so my legs are longer.

I got to the bathroom right before she did. "I won," I said.

"Girls, it's too late for such crazy running," Mom said. She was standing in the bathroom doorway. Her feet were actually in the bathroom, but her belly was so big it stuck out the bathroom door. She was like a real-life version of the chocolate Buddhas they sell at the store. Behind her, the water was running into the tub. It was almost filled up to the amount of water I like to have in the bath.

"Stella started it," Penny said.

I was going to tell Penny she couldn't talk because I said jinx, but it was actually good she talked because she called me Stella. "See, I am Stella!" I said. "You called me Stella!"

"I meant Sherry," Penny said. "You made me mess up. You know I'm Stella now!"

"One of my Stellas needs to get into the tub pronto," Mom said. She walked over to turn the faucet off. The water was at the perfect level.

"I'll get in," I said.

"No, I will," Penny said. "I always take my bath first."

It was true—Penny did always take the first bath, because I was older and my bedtime was later. Penny started getting undressed right there in the hall. "I have to go, but you have to flush," she told Mom.

"All right," Mom said.

"When you said Stella, who did you mean—me or her?" I asked.

"Well, I meant Penny," Mom said. "You told me you wanted to be called Sherry, and your sister said she wouldn't answer unless I called her Stella."

"See, I told you," Penny said, and she stuck out her tongue.

"Penelope Jane," Mom said, using Penny's full, old name—the way she does when she's mad.

Dad came down the hall right then. "What is this ruckus?" he asked. 'Ruckus' is one of my favorite words—it means something noisy is going on. But right then I didn't care about my words. I stuck my tongue out at Penny, and then I ran back down before Mom could say "Stella Rae."

I went to my room. I felt so confused. I didn't even like the name Stella. At least I used to not like it, so why did I miss it so much?

Dad knocked on my door—he always remembers to knock. "What's wrong, darling?" he asked.

I shrugged my shoulders. "Penny stuck her tongue out at me," I said.

"Penny does silly things sometimes," he said. "She's only five. I'm sure she didn't mean it."

I nodded. I am eight, and I still do silly things. Like changing my name was a really silly idea. Scheherazade was long and had too many syllables, and it was hard to remember that it was even my name. It was so much easier when I had just one name—my old name. I was Stella, and Penny was Penny, and Willa was Willa, and Lucy was Lucy. There weren't any new names to remember, and I never messed up.

"Is something else bothering you, darling?" Dad asked. "Oops, I'm supposed to call you Sherry now, right?"

"I just want some privacy," I said.

"Sure thing," Dad said. "I'm here if you need me."

This is my trick I sometimes do when I'm upset: I close my eyes and picture Batts Confections in my head. It just makes me feel better to think about all that candy—gummy bears, Junior Mints, Hershey's Kisses, the M&M rainbow, jelly bean jewelry, candy crayons, the Penny Candy Wall, Stella's Fudge.

So then I was back to the name Stella, and I opened my eyes. I said my name—my old name—over and over again in my head. Stella. Stella. Stella. It was sort of a good name after all. In my book, I call myself Stella. And the sign on my door still says Stella's Room. I shouldn't even care what Joshua said. He is just a meanie. Nobody even listens to him.

I clicked my heels together three times. I wished I'd never changed my name.

Mom came in to get me for my bath. Penny was behind her, wrapped up in a towel. "I can wash my hair and sing at the same time," she said.

"So? I'm still mad at you," I told her.

"You said I could be Stella," Penny reminded me. "No backsies."

"That's not what no backsies is," I told her. "You only use no backsies when you're giving something away that you don't want back. But I want my name back."

"Mom," Penny said. She started stamping her feet. "It's not fair. She gets all the good names."

"Penny is a good name," Mom said. "It's a beautiful name. It's one of my favorite names."

"No, it's stinky. She shouldn't get two

good names. I want to be Stella or Sherry."

"You can be Sherry," I said. "I'm just going to be Stella."

"You are?" Mom asked.

I nodded. "It's too hard to have a new name. I'm used to being Stella."

"I think you're a perfect Stella," Mom said. "The thing about your name is that it's your very own name. Daddy and I picked it out for you, and no one can take it away."

"If Stella is just going to be Stella then I'm just going to be Penny," Penny said. "So now you can't be mad at me anymore."

"I'm not," I said.

"Good," Mom said. "The Batts girls have to stick together. Remember, we have a little boy coming soon."

"I'm never going to want a boy's name," Penny said.

"Me neither," I said. "I'm never going to want any name except Stella."

"Dad, come in here!" Penny yelled. "We have something to tell you!"

Dad came back to my room. He knocked on my door because that's what the sign says.

"Come in!" I called.

"We're Penny and Stella again," Penny

told him. "I'm Penny and she's Stella, just like you picked out for us."

"Oh, thank goodness. I was having a hard time remembering who was who," Dad said.

"Me too," Mom said.

"Me three," I said.

"Not me," Penny said. "I always remembered, except for that one time. But I'm going to be Penny from now on anyway."

So then I had my name back. When I finish this book, it'll say "By Stella Batts" across the cover. One day I might write another book. I think it would be really cool if the name Stella Batts ends up meaning someone who's a really great storyteller—maybe even the best storyteller ever. But for now this is the end of the story.

Epilogue

(that means what happens after the end):

Here is a list of some more things that happened.

1. After a few days, the kids at school went back to their old names. It was just easier that way. Besides, Mrs. Finkel would only use our real names anyway.

2. Miss Linka came back to the lunchroom. All of us kids hope she never goes on vacation ever again.

3. Mom and Dad changed their mind about the baby's name. Now's he's going to be named Cooper. There really isn't a good nickname for Cooper, but Mom and Dad love the name. Dad says they're going to come up with something really great at Batts Confections to name after him.

Sneak preview of

Stella Batts

Hair Today, Gone Tomorrow

Book

A List of Really Awful Things That Happen When You Wake Up and There's Gum in Your Hair

1. At first you don't even know what happened. Something just feels different.

2. You sit up and reach your hand to your cheek, which is the place where it feels the weirdest. Then you find out that the reason it feels so weird is because your hair is stuck there. And the reason that your hair is stuck there is because you went to sleep with gum in your mouth, and sometime in the middle of the night, the gum fell out of your mouth and landed in your hair.

 Your little sister comes into your room without knocking—even though she's supposed to knock since there's a sign on your door that says, This is Stella's Room. If You Are Not Stella Then Please Knock—and she turns on the lights and says, "What happened to your hair? It's sticking out on the sides, like Pippi Longstocking!"

 So you go over to the big mirror, and your sister follows you because she's always following you and copying you. Your hair is all bunched up in a clump by the left side of your face.

 Your sister says, "Hey, that's gum in your

hair!" And then she says she'll go wake up your parents so they can help get it out. But you're not supposed to wake your parents up before 8:00 AM on weekends, unless it's an emergency.

6. Besides you don't want your parents to know about the gum because then they'll figure out you chewed it after bedtime, which is also not allowed.

7. At first you try and pull the clump out, but it hurts to pull your own hair. Even when you press one hand on top of your head, right by the roots, the way your mom does when she's brushing the knots out of your hair, it still hurts a lot. And anyway, the gum is super stuck.

8. You get your art scissors, because you think maybe you can cut the gum out. It's just there on the side, right by the edge of your bangs. So if you cut it, it will just look like you have a little bit more bangs.

9. Once you have the scissors, you sit down right in front of the mirror and get to work. For an eensy weensy piece of gum, it sure is stuck to a lot of your hair. You make sure to cut so it matches up with the bangs you already have.

10. Then your sister brings over the princess mirror so you can hold it up the way they do at the hair salon and see all the angles. You notice that the bangs on the left side go back on your head a little more than the ones on the right, so you decide to even it out.

11. As you are trimming some more your sister says, "I think you're cutting too much."

12. You look in the mirror and see that she's right: you have way too many bangs. They go all the way around to right by your ears, and you look so ugly that you wish you could scoop back all the hair on the floor and make it stick back to your head.

13. When you start to cry your sister says, "I'm waking up Mom and Dad. This is definitely an emergency."

Courtney Sheinmel

Courtney Sheinmel is the author of several books for middle grade readers, including *Sincerely* and *All The Things You Are*. Like Stella Batts, she was born in California and has a younger sister, but unlike Stella, her parents never owned a candy store. Now Courtney lives in New York City, where she has tasted all the cupcakes in her neighborhood. She also makes a delicious cookie brownie graham cracker pie. Visit her online at www. courtneysheinmel.com, where you can find the recipe along with information about upcoming Stella Batts books.

Jennifer A. Bell

Jennifer A. Bell is a children's book illustrator whose work can also be found in magazines, on greeting cards, and on the occasional Christmas ornament. She studied Fine Arts at the Columbus College of Art and Design and currently lives in Minneapolis, Minnesota.

In this early chapter book series, the ups and downs of Stella's life are charmingly chronicled. She's in third grade, she wants to be a writer, and her parents own a candy shop. Life should be sweet, right?

Read more about Stella in

Stella Batts

Stella Batts, Hair Today, Gone Tomorrow

Stella Batts Pardon Me

Stella Batts A Case of the Meanies

Stella Batts Who's in Charge?